# Why Is My Dad
# Mad At Me?

# Why Is My Dad Mad At Me?

PATRICIA H. MAYNARD

authorHOUSE®

AuthorHouse™
1663 Liberty Drive
Bloomington, IN 47403
www.authorhouse.com
Phone: 1-800-839-8640

Published by AuthorHouse    01/08/2015

ISBN: 978-1-4969-2804-7 (sc)
ISBN: 978-1-4969-2803-0 (hc)
ISBN: 978-1-4969-4297-5 (e)

Library of Congress Control Number: 2014917365

Illustrated by Jean Bray

# Contents

Part One

My Childhood and Natural Curiosity.............................1

Part Two

Father and Son Bonding Time.................................27

Part Three

Playing with childhood Buddies/Involving the
Neighbor.....................................................................55

Part Four

Dad's future Plans for me/ My Choice/ My
graduation................................................................77

To my husband, Paul Maynard, MD; my three sons, Dwight, Dwayne, and Paul; and to the Know It and Grow It Boys' Gardening Club. You were my motivation and inspiration for writing this book.

I established the gardening club to encourage the boys to build their knowledge and skills in that area. I also wanted to provide a hands-on opportunity for the boys to interact socially, to build their teamwork skills, and to help them develop their dreams and careers.

# Part One

## My Childhood and Natural Curiosity

I enjoyed the days and nights when my parents read to me. They took turns. Dad read at my request, and mom usually read my bedtime stories. My favorite books were about Curious George. They all made me laugh, and I would beg to hear more. I wondered why this monkey did the things he did.

When I learned to read by myself, I would read my collection of Curious George books over and over again. I noticed I was very curious too. I was always asking, "Why, Dad?" or "Why, Mom?"

Sometimes when my dad got tired of my questions, he said, "Go look for the answers, and then let me know what you find out."

One day, I responded, "But why can't you give me the answer?"

He replied, "That's how you will learn, Son!"

I said, "Okay, Dad, I will learn."

My mother would say, "Let's go find out together."

My first set of curious experiences took place when I was between the ages of six and eight years old. My dad would take a radio with him when he sat outside so he could listen to the news or sports. He loved baseball, specifically the Yankees. When his team played, he shouted and cheered. I sat next to him and imitated his actions. I pumped my fist and shouted, "Yes!" Sometimes I brought my arm down with such force that I elbowed my ribs. Ouch! Even though it hurt, I loved being with my father.

One day Dad had to work late, so I decided to listen to the radio by myself. I climbed on a chair and took the radio down from above the refrigerator. I walked out on the porch, sat in dad's favorite chair, and turned on the radio. I heard a booming voice say, "Let him go! That is not fair." I picked up the radio and put it to my ear. The man repeated the same thing. I looked at it and turned it back and forth, thinking this man sounded as big as my dad. How did he get into the little radio? How could I help him get out? I tried turning and twisting the radio to take it apart, but that didn't work. Then I remembered where my dad kept his toolbox. I ran inside and opened it, looking for the screwdriver. I had seen my dad using it before and I asked what kind of tool it was and what he used it for. I was glad I had asked him so many questions, because now I knew how to help the big man get out of the little radio. I thought he must have been all squeezed up inside of it.

I picked up the screwdriver, remembering how my dad used it. I put it into the head of each screw, turning and twisting each one, until the device fell apart. I looked at all the pieces. I looked inside and outside. I did not find the man, and I didn't hear his voice anymore. He must have jumped out when I wasn't looking. I took the radio apart, piece by piece. I wanted to make sure the little man was not trapped under any of the little parts. But he was nowhere to be found. I was so puzzled. I was just about to go ask mom what had happened when I saw dad walking through the gate. I looked at him and then at his radio in many pieces on a chair. I ran to meet him and said, "Dad, you won't believe what happened!"

He replied, "What happened, son?" So, I explained that I heard a man in the radio. Dad kept walking as I talked, and as he stepped on the porch, he saw his radio stripped apart. He stopped, stared at it, and then said. "Vendel, what happened to the radio? Did you drop it?"

"No, Dad! This is what I was trying to tell you." I started the story all over again. He picked up the pieces, sat down, shook his head, and tried to put the pieces back together.

He held up the screwdriver and asked, "Where did you learn to use this?

I replied, "I watched you use it and asked about it."

"Yes! Now I remember. I am happy you learned something from me, but your curious mind will get you into trouble if you aren't careful. Son, I want you to promise me something."

"What, Dad?" I felt relieved that I was not going to receive a spanking, so I was eager to make any promise. I repeated my question. "What did you want me to promise?"

He replied, "When you grow up and get your first job, you will buy me a radio."

"Oh! Yes, Dad, I will buy you a radio, a watch, a car, a house, and anything else you and Mom want." My parents were good to me, so I knew I would always be good to them. This adventure with the radio and others like it taught me for sure that I had curiosity, a vivid imagination, and an above-average brain.

I always asked questions, but I didn't always wait for the answers. I tried to discover things for myself. My dad can confirm this. He told anyone who would listen about the day I smashed his watch. I was about six years old, staying home from school because I had the sniffles and I was coughing uncontrollably. The day before, I had come home from school with a fever and a headache. I kept my mom up all night. I was restless and felt miserable. She tried everything, including baby aspirin, bush tea, and resting cold rags on my forehead. She also rubbed my back and chest with one of her custom mixtures. After walking back and forth to check on me several times, she wrapped me in a thick blanket and crawled into bed with me. I hugged her tightly and drifted off to sleep.

The next morning, I woke up feeling a lot better, but my mom decided to keep me home. I didn't mind, even though some of the homemade medicines tasted awful. I knew I would also receive treats like ice cream, ice pops, and lollipops. I took advantage of this, calling from my room, "Mom, can you bring me some more juice, please? Thank you. Oh, Mom, can I have ice cream after lunch? But I think I will have a Popsicle now."

Mom responded, "Okay, Vendel you can have one after you take your medicine." Right away, I knew that meant I was going to get some unpleasant-tasting stuff. Sure enough, Mom was back in a flash, carrying a spoon and a jar of something my grandmother gave her. She claimed it was the best treatment for colds and flus. My mom gave me a spoonful, and I almost vomited. I needed all my treats at once. Mom was pleased when I swallowed it down, so she gave me a Popsicle right away.

"Thanks, Mom! Do I have to take any more?" She laughed and left the room. After all of these treatments, I got out of bed. I really felt better. As usual, I looked for something to do.

I wandered into my parent's room, and dad's new watch was on the nightstand. I picked it up and held it to one ear. I heard the ticking sound. I took it away from my ear, looked at it, and then I put it back up to my ear and heard the same ticktack. I pulled it away again and looked at the hands. I thought about the nursery rhyme I had learned in kindergarten that said, "Hickory dickory dock, the mouse ran up the clock. The clock struck one, the mouse ran down ..." Suddenly, my mind raced. I saw the long hand pointing to the twelve and the short hand pointing to the one. Any minute, the mouse was going to get out, and I didn't want him to. I wanted to see why he was making the ticking sound in my dad's watch. I ran and got one of my mom's thick-heeled shoes—I think she calls them clogs. I came back, picked up the watch, and listened again. I still heard the ticktack. I turned the watch on its side and hit it so hard that it smashed open, and parts flew everywhere. I wasn't worried about that; I could put them back together, or so I thought. I just wanted to find the mouse. I thought, *I guess he was so tiny that I smashed him into bits.* I couldn't find him anywhere to ask, "Why did you make that tick tock, and why did you choose to run down at one?" I sat on the floor and cried as I tried to put my dad's watch back together. I knew I was in serious trouble, so I wanted to run away and hide. I got my school glue and tried to stick the tiny pieces together.

Just then, I heard my mom call, "Vendel! Vendel! It is time for lunch!" She walked into the room, and with a trained eye, she instantly saw the mess I had made. She said, "Why did you touch your father's watch? What did you do to it? You are in serious trouble now. The other day, it was the radio. Tell me what you were doing with the watch." I told her about the sound I heard and recited the rhyme for her.

She looked at me and burst out laughing. But then her face got serious, and she said, "Your father is so old-fashioned. I told him to buy a digital watch, but he said, 'No, I love this one. I had a hard time finding it and I intend to keep it even if I can't find someone who knows how to repair it.'"

Your dad was so proud of that watch. He only removes it when he takes a shower. Last night, I finally got him to take it off and place it on the nightstand. He woke up late this morning and had to rush off. I guess he forgot it. We will both be in trouble for this. Vendel, you are going to school tomorrow no matter how sick you are. Take your curiosity there! Go explore and learn all you can there!"

I ran over to my mom, hugged her, and said, "Mom, please don't be mad at me! I just wanted to find out what made the sound and why."

She hugged me and said, "Okay, Son, let's go eat lunch."

After lunch, I took a nap. As I slept, I dreamed that I was the captain of a spaceship. My team and I were flying to Mars. I told them about all the things we might find there, such as people who were all colors of the rainbow: red, orange, yellow, green, blue, purple. I explained that the people living on Mars were these specific colors because of the fruits they ate, and that is all they had to eat. They asked me too many questions, and I told them to stop. I had to concentrate on landing the ship correctly so we didn't end up in an apple orchard, an orange grove, or a pineapple patch. They all laughed. Just as the spaceship was about to touch the ground, I heard what I thought was thunder. It was actually my father's loud voice. "Vendel, get out here now!"

My eyes flew open, and I jumped out of bed. I shouted, "I am coming, Dad! I have to use the bathroom!"

He responded, "Hurry and get out here!" My knees felt weak, my heart was beating fast, and it felt like the pee would run down my legs if I didn't hustle to the bathroom. I used the bathroom quickly but took my time washing my hands. I heard that thunderous voice again. "Vendel, do I need to come in there and get you?" I shut off the faucet and walked quickly to the bedroom. My dad stood next to the nightstand, and my mom sat on the bed, her hands propped up under her chin.

I said, "Yes, Dad, I am here."

"Tell me what you did to my watch."

"I was just trying to find out what was happening inside your watch." I explained to him the sounds I heard and how the nursery rhyme I remembered got me even more curious. My dad listened, staring at me intently, and then he reached out his hand. I thought he was going to grab me and give me the beating of my life, but instead he rested his hand gently on my shoulder and pulled me to him.

He said, "Son, even though this was my favorite watch and I loved it so much, when I think about what you said, I have to forgive you for this one." I was so shocked that I stared at him with my eyes and mouth wide open. He added, "Do you want to know why? I did the same thing to my father—your grandfather. I guess you have that natural curiosity like me. It is in your genes you inherit that." I breathed a sigh of relief then I climbed into the bed next to my mom. She looked more relaxed and even had a smile on her face, which was very reassuring to me.

I imagined she was thinking, "Whew! He got away with this one."

I said, "Mom, it's time to eat!"

As mom and I walked out of the bedroom, I looked back and saw dad still holding his watch, shaking his head and muttering, "That boy! I wonder what he will become one day. This is another item he will have to repay me for."

There was another time I read in my science book about mixing colors to get different shades, and curiosity got the better of me, as usual. I wanted to try it out, and I remembered my mom had a box of food coloring in the cupboard. She had bought it to make a rainbow cake for my birthday. I thought, *Oh well! She will just have to get another one. I need to know which two colors will give me yellow. What two colors give me green? Which ones make brown?* The ideas, questions, and plans continued to whirl around in my mind.

I got the box of food coloring and several of my mom's small bowls, but I decided to put the bowls away. I got some plastic cups instead so that just in case I furthered my typical sort of experiment, I wouldn't damage the dishes. It didn't make any sense to be in trouble with both my mom and dad. I found out red and blue made green, red and yellow made orange, and red and blue made purple. I was pleased with my discoveries. Just as I was about to create my own concoction, my mom came into the kitchen. "Vendel, what are you up to now? Clean up your mess and get out of my kitchen." I agreed. There would be other times to experiment.

Science and math were my best subjects. I got As and sometimes an A plus. There was always something new to learn and ask questions about in science class. When I entered the science fair in sixth grade, I won first place. Using my skills in math and science, I made an airplane model and took the judges through my process step by step. I felt so proud of myself, and I displayed my trophy and ribbon on my dresser. In seventh grade, I prepared for the science fair again. I knew what I wanted to do and spent weeks researching my experiment. I learned the basic parts of the computer and wrote each one and its function on index cards as follows:

1) **Processor**—the brain of the computer.

2) **Motherboard**—connects all the other parts.

3) **Case**—holds all the parts together.

4) **RAM**—random-access memory.

5) **Graphics Card**—takes care of displaying the graphics.

6) **Hard Drive**—stores all the data.

7) **Optical Drive**—the CD or DVD drive.

8) **Power Supply**—provides electricity to all the components.

I also made diagrams and charts. I studied them daily, and then I was ready to assemble a computer. When I told my dad that my science project was to build a computer from scratch, he looked at me and said, "Son, please don't take apart the one in the house."

I explained, "No, Dad, we can order the parts to build it."

My dad let out a sigh of relief and said, "Get all the information, and we will place the order." I was so excited to hear him say this. I ran into the house and navigated to a website, and then I called for my dad. He came with his credit card and paid for the order with all the computer parts.

I jumped up and hugged my dad, shook his hand, and said, "Dad, you are a good man!" He let out a hearty laugh that told me he was pleased. I couldn't wait for my computer parts to come. I studied and rehearsed the process over and over while the pieces were on their way. I counted down the days until I would be able to get my hands on the project. I also rehearsed the speech that I would wow the judges with. Even though I knew it would take three weeks for the order to arrive, I checked the mailbox every day when I came home from school. Mom looked at me and smiled.

By the time the package arrived, the science fair was on the following Friday. I locked myself in my room; pulled out my maps, diagrams, and notes; and got busy. I spent hours putting things together and testing them. Sometimes my mom had to remind me to eat. My dad peeked in and asked, "Son, how is it coming along?" I would respond with a thumbs-up, and he would close the door with a smile. I finished my project, tested it out, and then invited my dad to use it. He was so impressed and excited that he shouted for my mom to come and look. My mom ran into the room and she too was elated.

She touched the keys, turned it around, looked at it, and said, "Vendel, you did this?"

My dad turned to her and asked, "What did you expect? This is my son!" I took my project to school the next day. My teacher and classmates all crowded around me as I explained my project and demonstrated it.

The day of the science fair, I got up early, ate my breakfast, and pestered Dad to drive me to school. My classmates all arrived with their usual projects: tornadoes, crystals, or magnets. I carefully boxed up my precious computer and display board with labeled diagrams. My speech was tucked away in my pocket in case I needed it for reference. I had rehearsed it several times that week, and I was ready to take on the challenge. Students from several other schools had entries on display too. The judges made their rounds and wrote briskly on their score sheets. They came over to the seventh grade section, and I was first in line. I stood up, welcomed them, and then made my presentation in a clear and authoritative voice. I also did the demonstration with a lot of self-confidence. I responded to their questions in detail. I also invited them to test my project. My teacher and classmates applauded after I finished. I felt good about myself, and winning first place was the only thing I thought about. They had one more group to judge before they announced the winners. As I waited, I remembered my mom had packed a sandwich for me. It tasted good, and it was my favorite: a peanut butter and jelly sandwich.

Just as I took the last bite, my teacher called out, "It's lunch time! Come get your lunches." She handed out bagged lunches from the cafeteria.

I took one and said, "Thank you!" I looked inside the bag, took out the apple and milk container for myself, and then gave the sandwich to my friend Elroy. Every day at lunch, he came to the cafeteria, ate his lunch, and then went back for seconds. He eventually got the nickname Seconds.

On my way to the bathroom, I saw a boy with a rocket he made from paper towel and toilet tissue tubes. I asked him about how he made it and told him I could help him launch it. He replied, "You can make it go up in the air?"

I said, "Yes!" I invited him over to my house and told him to bring the rocket. We exchanged numbers, and then I walked briskly to the bathroom. I didn't want to miss the winners being announced. I was standing at the urinal when Seconds burst into the bathroom. He blurted out, "Vendel! You are the first-place winner." I quickly pulled up my zipper, ran to the sink, washed my hands, and ran out of the bathroom. I saw my science teacher heading to the stage as the judges kept calling my name. I sped up and reached the stage before her. Everyone laughed and cheered loudly. I rushed up to the podium and received a trophy, a certificate, and a firm handshake from Mr. Esdaille, the science coordinator. I asked him if I could have the microphone, and he gave it to me. I thanked the judges and then called up my science teacher, Mrs. Mills.

I gave her a big hug and said, "Thank you!" I beamed with pride and held my trophy high as I left the stage. *Yes! I won first prize in the science fair.* I felt proud of myself. I had to agree with my teacher and my parents: When you study and work hard, you will do well.

# Part Two

## Father and Son Bonding Time

When my dad decided it was time for me to do bonding activities with him, he would challenge me to some kind of sports or take me fishing. I was eight years old the first time this happened, he took me outside to play basketball with a new hoop he had set up. He said, "I'll let you make the first shot." I dribbled the ball, passed it between my legs, and then prepared to take a jump shot. He suddenly slapped the ball away from me and took the shot. This made me angry. I ran over to the ball, picked it up, jumped, and made a slam dunk. Before dad could pick up the ball, I grabbed it and slam-dunked it again. My dad stood there and looked at me with his hands on his hips as I picked up the basketball and walked back toward the house. I heard shuffling sounds behind me, so I glanced over my shoulder and saw my dad running behind me. I rushed up the stairs, but one of my shoelaces was untied. I tripped and fell down, and one knee hit the edge of the stairs. I yelled and kept holding the ball, trying to hop into the house.

When my mom heard me howling, she ran to the door and asked, "What's wrong?" She held on to me and tried to help me inside.

My dad shouted, "Just leave him alone. Don't baby him—he is a man. He needs to be tough." My mom didn't listen to him. She put her hand around my waist and helped me to a chair, and then she used a cotton swab with peroxide to dab on my injured knee as I moaned and groaned. My dad yelled, "Why didn't you clean it with alcohol?"

I responded, "No! That would hurt more."

My mom replied, "Son, I won't do anything to hurt you. I love you too much." She kissed me on the cheek, and my knee started to feel better right away.

My dad walked over to my mom and asked, "Where is my kiss?" My mom turned and gave him a quick peck on the cheek. Then my dad turned to me and said, "Okay, Son, it was a bit rough for you today, but you have to toughen up and develop good sportsmanship." Then he rubbed my head and walked into the kitchen. I laughed as I saw my mom carrying a tray with my dinner and my dad following close behind with my drink and dessert. I knew they loved me no matter what happened.

The next father-son bonding time was one Monday after one Easter when dad decided he would teach me to play cricket. He told me that it was the number-one Caribbean team sport. He also explained that each of the two teams is made up of eleven players. The bat has a flat side, and the ball is about the size of a baseball but much harder. He got his bat and ball out of the closet and said, "You have to learn this game. Your uncles and I played it when we were your age and older. You are going to love it. Let me give you a demonstration."

When we were outside, he stood in a hunched position and started swinging the bat back, and then he leaned back on one leg and took a good swing. He looked at me and said, "Ah! Boy, I've still got it!"

I asked, "Got what, Dad?"

He replied, "My best swing." Then he said, "Pick up the ball, and throw it to me as if you were throwing a softball." I lifted my leg, turned, and let the ball go with force. I watched the ball spin out of control as it left my hand. My dad picked up the bat and leaned back, and then I heard my dad repeatedly yell, "Ow!" He dropped the bat and held his hand up as he jumped and spun around. I saw blood coming from his thumb, his face showed he was in pain. I tried to speak, but no words came out.

I walked over, and looked at him for a while and then said, "Sorry, Dad!" He kept holding his thumb and just looked at me. But then I remembered how he leaped into the air, and I couldn't help myself. I dropped to the ground and laughed uncontrollably. After I recovered from this, I looked up at Dad and saw a tear roll down his cheek. I said, "Are you crying, Dad? Tough men don't cry! Let's go in the house and take care of it."

I helped him into the house and yelled for mom. He sat at the kitchen table, still holding his injured thumb. I said, "All right, Dad, do I get ice or the rubbing alcohol?" When I stepped toward the bathroom to get the alcohol, he finally got his ability to speak back.

He said, "Boy, don't bring the alcohol out here! That would make my finger hurt more. Bring the ice." I responded, "Oh dad you remembered when I hurt my knee you wanted mom to use the alcohol. So you did know it would hurt more? So now it's you, you can't take the pain? Ha! Ha!"

My mom heard the conversation and she couldn't control her laughter. Then she said, "I will take care of it. You know your dad can be a big baby sometimes."

My dad had advice for everyone but he did not take it himself. Mom brought a cup holding a saltwater solution and told Dad to soak his thumb in it. He did, but after thirty seconds, he pulled it back out quickly and shouted, "I can't take the pain." After a second or two, Mom cleaned his wound with peroxide, put some ointment on it, and then bandaged it. Dad kept moaning and groaning as mom nursed his finger.

Dad played other sports with me, but he never invited me to play cricket with him again. However, he took me to several cricket matches. We even traveled to watch what he called test games. I was interested in watching the game, but I knew for sure that I didn't want to play it. I couldn't help chuckling quietly when I remembered my dad's reaction to getting hit. I told him how sorry I was and that I not did want the same thing to happen to me. He laughed and said, "Son, you can get hurt in any sport."

For our next father-son bonding time, Dad called me to his room one Friday night and said, "Vendel, tomorrow is Saturday. I don't have to go to work, so we will go fishing. I will teach you how. I have already bought the rods, reels, line, hooks, and bait. In fact, the tackle box is all put together." I really wanted to go on the fishing trip.

I thought, *I hope I catch a big fish. I know my mom will cook it well. We will probably have fish and fungi for dinner. Fungi is a dish made from steamed cornmeal with or without okra.*

I was so excited that I couldn't sleep. My dad said we would leave early the next morning. This would let us catch the fish when they were hungry.

I planned to put a lot of bait on my hook. If the fish was hungry, it would take a big bite and get hooked. I smiled as I thought about my plan and how well it would work. I would show Dad that I could catch my own fish—I could be a fisher. I finally drifted off to sleep with fishing on my mind.

I dreamed that as dad and I were standing on a rock to fish, a big wave splashed us. My foot slipped, and I fell into the water. I looked up and saw a giant fish swimming toward me. It looked like a shark. I swam in the other direction, and as I opened my mouth to shout, my mouth filled with water. I felt like I was drowning. I spat out the water and swam faster. I looked back, and the big fish was still close behind me. As I got to the rock, the big fish opened its mouth and swallowed me up. I closed my eyes tightly as I felt my body get pushed down inside. I realized it might have been a whale. A shark's sharp teeth would have ripped my skin.

I remembered the story of Jonah that my Sunday school teacher had told me. I prayed, "Dear Lord, please let me be a Jonah so that this whale will spit me out whole on the shore, next to my father. We want to continue fishing. I want to catch a big fish for dinner." As I said this, I felt myself been pushed further into the whale's body. I went past the esophagus and down into the stomach. I saw and smelled everything fishy in there: seaweed, fish, squid, and tiny ocean creatures. There was plenty of room for all of us. I wondered what type of whale I was inside. I prayed louder. If it swallowed anything or anyone else, I might get crushed or squeezed, and then I wouldn't be able to get out. With what seemed like my last breath, I raised my hands in the air and shouted, "Lord, hear my prayer!" I felt like I was being pulled out of the whale.

Suddenly, I heard my dad's voice. "Come on, Vendel! Time to get up and go fishing." As I opened my eyes, my dad was pulling me up and out of the bed. I was so relieved to find out that I was not in the belly of a whale. My dad let go of me, and I sat up in bed, rubbed my eyes, and headed for the bathroom. After I changed into my fishing clothes, I went to the kitchen. My mom was packing our cooler with lunch and snacks for dad and me. I peeked in and saw all the goodies I liked. A smile crept across my face, and my heartbeat got faster with excitement. I was ready for the fishing trip. Dad loaded the gear, and I put the cooler in the car. We said good-bye to Mom, and then we were off. As we drove, I told Dad about my dream. He laughed and then said, "Boy, you have such a vivid imagination. You think big! You dream big! You are going to grow up to do great things. I have big plans for you."

I responded, "Really, Dad?"

He said, "Yes, you have big shoes to fill, so hurry up and grow up." He continued, "Your granddad took me fishing on Friday nights. Sometimes, we would stay all night and not even catch one fish. We sat on the beach and talked. In fact, he would do most of the talking. When I fell asleep, he would wake me up and say, 'Son, every day is a fishing day, but not every day is a catching day. Let's go home.' I would walk back home with him, feeling so disappointed. However, I always looked forward to the Friday night we went fishing. We had many good nights. And I hope you and I will have a good day today."

I replied, "I hope so too." I wanted my dad to be proud of me. I planned to catch lots of fish.

When we got to the beach, my dad looked for a spot shaded by the sea grape trees. He told me to put the cooler down and get the tackle box. Next, he brought the reels and showed me how to hook the bait. He said, "Son, make sure your bait is secure. Step back, snap your rod forward, and roll out your line. Wait till you feel a fish bite, and then reel it in." I listened intently and followed the instructions.

I stood on the beach and waited patiently. Dad asked, "Do you feel any tugs on your line?"

I responded, "No! Not yet."

He replied, "You will soon!" I watched dad cast his line. He leaned back and then snapped it forward. I thought I would do it that way the next time. Suddenly, I heard Dad shout, "I have one! I think it is a big one. I am reeling it in—I can feel it resisting, but I've got it." My dad turned the handle on his reel really fast, and I watched intently to see the big fish. As Dad struggled and reeled in his catch, he raised it higher. We looked at the end of the line, and we were both shocked at what we saw.

I pointed and shouted, "Look, Dad, you caught an old pair of jeans!" We sat down on the sand. I laughed, while Dad pulled and tugged to get the pants untangled.

After a few minutes, he said, "Son, pass me the knife so that I can cut the line and get this darn thing off my line." I opened the tackle box and gave my dad the knife like he requested. With one forceful swipe, he cut the line and tossed the old jeans aside. As I sat and watched him attach new bait to his line, my mind wandered. I thought about the old pair of jeans and who they belonged to.

I thought, *What if the person drowned or a shark ate him or her?* I thought about my dream and got scared.

I asked, "Dad, don't you think we should try a different spot? The fish don't seem to be biting."

He cast his line, turned to me, and said, "Boy, this is the best spot. They will start biting soon. Get some fresh bait and throw out your line again."

I did what he told me to, and then I waited for a while, holding my fishing pole firmly. I felt a tug, and I tried to pull my line. It felt like it was snapping.

I called, "Dad, come and help me! I think I have a big one."

He replied, "Boy, you might have caught an old shoe." We both laughed, but my line and reel were slipping out of my hand. When dad saw this, he put down his rod and came to help me. He took the rod from me and started reeling it in. He said, "Vendel, you are right. Look what we have here: a big snapper." The fish twisted and turned as my dad lifted it out of the water.

I said, "Dad, let me have the line. This is my fish. I caught him, so I want to bring him in."

When Dad had reeled the fish almost to shore, he said, "Now you can reel it in." I grabbed my rod and turned the handle fast as the fish thrashed around in the sand.

"What do I do now, Dad?" I asked excitedly.

Dad grabbed the fish by the tail and unhooked it from the line. He said, "Here is your fish!" I was afraid to touch it because I thought it might bite me. After a while, I picked it up and threw it in our fishing bag. It was about the length of my arm. I felt good! I had caught my first fish, and Dad hadn't caught anything yet. I smiled to myself, looked around to see if dad was watching, and then I patted myself on the back. I couldn't wait to get home to show Mom my catch and tell her what I wanted for dinner. Thinking about food made me feel hungry, so I went to the cooler and took out two sandwiches and a bottle of lemonade. I sat down and ate as I watched Dad snap his rod in different areas, trying to catch a fish.

When he looked over at me, I said, "Dad, come and eat. These sandwiches are delicious!"

He replied, "Not yet, Son. You got your dinner, but I still have to catch mine."

I responded, "All right, Dad! Make sure you get a bigger one than mine."

He said, "I will, Vendel. You wait and see."

I waited for hours, and it didn't happen. I caught two smaller fish that I was able to reel in by myself. Each time I felt a bite on my line, I shouted and jumped up and down excitedly.

My dad said, "Boy, stop the noise. You are scaring away the fish." But I couldn't help it. When I felt the third fish on my line, I screamed even louder than before. I know for sure that it would scare anyone or anything around. I thought, *I am becoming quite a fisher.*

Dad looked at my catch and said, "I can do better than that." Then I reminded him of my big fish in the bag. He continued fishing but didn't catch anything more. I told him there was always a next time.

He said I should say what my granddad always said: "Every day is a fishing day, but not every day is a catching day." My dad said that if I repeated the phrase, we could go home, so I did. He sat down, packed up his tackle box, ate a couple of sandwiches, and drank some lemonade and a bottle of water.

Then he said, "Son, it is time to go home." We picked up our gear and went back to the car. Before dad started the engine, he said, "Now, don't go home and boast to your mom about being better at fishing than me. Sometimes you can get out of hand. Please don't make me look bad. Your mother will have a good laugh at me." I listened, but I did not make him any promises, because I knew I was going to brag when I got home. Instead of giving him the type of assurance he wanted, I distracted him by asking, "Dad, did we get everything? Oh, what about those old jeans that you caught? We should take them off the beach and throw them away so that if a big wave came up; they won't get washed back into the sea."

Dad replied, "Why did you have to remind me of that? I guess you are right, though."

Dad got out of the car, went back to the beach, and got the jeans. He put them in the trunk of the car, and then we drove away. I could tell Dad was deep in thought as he drove, so I didn't say anything. Then I asked, "Dad, are you mad at me?"

He said, "No, Vendel, I am not. I was thinking about your granddad. I have many memories of him. Coming here today, with you, brought them back. Son, I want you to keep this tradition alive and pass it on."

I answered attentively, "Yes, Dad! I will pass it on to my children"

As dad pulled up to the house, I jumped out and headed toward the house. I heard my dad call, "Vendel! Where are you going so fast? You have to take the stuff out of the trunk!" I ran back to the car and grabbed our gear and the fish. Mom opened the door as I walked up the steps. Dad was right behind me, so I decided to wait until he went to get cleaned up to tell her everything. Dad brushed past Mom, quickly saying, "Hi, dear," as he headed for the restroom. Mom and I went into the kitchen, and I took out my two little fish first.

She laughed and said, "I guess we have to cook something else for dinner. I have okra and cornmeal ready to make the fungi, but I will make the change." She looked so disappointed that I couldn't wait any longer to pull out my big red snapper. Then I saw something that warmed my heart: a big smile on my mom's face. I loved to see my mom happy. I guess she used her beautiful smile to win my dad's heart.

I told Mom my story, and she was pleased that I caught all the fish. She squeezed me tightly in a hug. Then I told her about the old pair of jeans Dad caught. She couldn't stop laughing and laughed even harder when I demonstrated how dad had struggled. She said, "Stop before you make me wet myself." She held her stomach as she continued to laugh.

I said, "Mom, you had better go to the bathroom before you make a mess on the kitchen floor." Then we laughed some more.

We were still having a good laugh when Dad walked into the kitchen. He said, "Okay, the joke is on me." Then he told Mom, "Hurry up and get my dinner ready. I can't wait to eat the snapper my son caught." My mom immediately turned on the burner. Then she reached into a drawer to get the fungi stick she would use to stir the cornmeal. My dad got up from the kitchen table, walked over to Mom, and said, "Let me see this. I have a good mind to use it on this boy. He promised not to tell you, but he did, and the two of you laughed at me." He grabbed the fungi stick and headed for me.

I jumped out of the chair where I was sitting and ran so fast that he couldn't catch me. I ran to my room and locked the door. I heard my mom shout, "Leave my son alone!"

My dad replied, "No! He has to feel something."

I shouted, "But, Dad. I didn't promise anything!"

He reached my door and hit it with the stick. I jumped back, as I was just about to open the door. He said, "Come out here, you little rat!" I was frightened. I wondered if I was going to finally get it for all the things I had done. My dad had never spanked me before, but maybe he was going to start now.

Then I heard my mom say, "Give me back my fungi stick so that I can stir my cornmeal." I waited to hear what would happen next. Then Dad said, "Come out, Son— open the door. I was only teasing you. Now the joke is on you because you ran away like a scared rabbit." After I heard his laughter, I knew it was safe to come out. My heart still felt like it was jumping out of my chest as I opened the door slowly. My dad stood there, big and tall. He held his arms open, and I walked into them. He hugged me and then patted me on the back and said, "Vendel, no matter what, I love you." It felt good to hear him say this. Dad rested his hand on my shoulder as we walked to the kitchen. I really felt his love. He was sincere.

I thought, *I have the best dad in the world.*

Mom stood by the kitchen table with her hands on her hips, and then she shook her head and smiled. Dad pulled a chair out for me and asked, "Honey, is dinner ready?" Mom walked over to the kitchen counter and placed the food on the table. The aroma of steamed snapper made me hungrier.

I picked up my fork, and as I was about to dig into it, my mom said, "Not so fast, Son. We have to thank God for this meal." She turned to Dad and asked, "Will you please bless the table? Don't forget to ask for a special blessing for our son." I put down my fork and bowed my head. Dad prayed as if he were trying to impress mom and me. The prayer was unusually long, and I couldn't wait to eat. I was just about to nudge Mom under the table when I heard Dad say, "Amen." Dad and I enjoyed the meal, and we expressed our thanks to my mom for cooking it.

# Part Three

## Playing with childhood Buddies/ Involving the Neighbor

The experiences I had with my dad, the boys in my neighborhood, and my classmates made me decide I didn't want to have a sports career. I was tall, stocky, and well-built. I could handle myself with any sport, or so I thought until some incidents reminded me I needed to stick to what I did best; reading books. The boys and I played tackle football. I was the first one to suggest it, and because of my size, I threw a lot of weight into every tackle. Sometimes I tackled them so hard I thought I would crush them to bits. In turn, they had a hard time taking me down. I always managed to get away. Most of them were average-sized boys, and some had small bodies and a slim build. However, Elroy was bigger and stockier than I was, but he could never tackle me by himself. I would always walk away from those football games feeling like a champion. I made all my attempted touchdowns and scored the most points. One day after school, my classmates invited me to stay after school to play my favorite game. I should have known something was unusual when I saw the way they begged after I told them I had to go home to research something. I finally agreed, and we threw our bags on the side of the field and took off our school uniforms. Some of my neighborhood friends were also around: Oliver, Vernon, and Vincent— who had lost a couple of front teeth playing the game. I also saw Marlon, who looked as if the wind could pick him up anytime. His nickname was Bag of Bones, but he could still play football well. He had long legs, so he could kick the ball past anyone. He always wanted to play, but if the game got really rough or if he got crushed by Stevie, Marlon ran home.

I thought these boys were there to cheer for me. Nothing was further from the truth. This was a game for them to take revenge, and everyone knew it but me.

The game started, and as usual, I took them down one by one. All my opponents on the other team couldn't score a touchdown. And then it was my turn with the ball, and I heard someone say, "Let's do it now!" I looked around, and the boys were coming from every angle. They rushed me with force that threw me to the ground. As I landed, I heard a loud snap and felt unbearable pain. I tried to push myself up, but all the boys—about twelve of them—were piled on top of me, so I couldn't move. I screamed in pain, but I still couldn't move. I couldn't take it any longer, so I drew a deep breath; arched up my back, and rocked back and forth. They finally toppled off of me. I used my last bit of strength to push myself up. Mr. Dallas, our physical education teacher, stood on the sidelines, watching the pile up. When he saw me crawling out of the pile, holding my arm up, he said, "That looks like a serious injury you have there." He tried to touch it, but I wouldn't let him. It was too painful. I said, "All right, fellows, you won this one." I felt like crying, but instead I walked home in agony.

My mom took me to the hospital, and the doctor in the emergency room sent me to an x-ray lab. They confirmed my arm was broken in two places, the wrist and the forearm. They put a cast on my arm and tied it in a sling. I also got some pain medicine.

My dad was upset about this. He didn't want anyone hurting his son, but he said, "Son, you took it like a man!"

My friends and I demonstrated the saying, "Boys will we be boys!" We often wrestled, fought, roughhoused, climbed, played ball, teased, and made fun of each other. Name any sort of aggressive play, and we did it.

The following incident took place with a neighbor at the end of my street, Mr. Brown. He was an elderly, no-nonsense gentleman, and he didn't approve of the behavior of some of the boys in the neighborhood. They were rude and disrespectful to their parents and to Mr. Brown. In fact, one of the boys had tried to rob him, but he managed to chase off the thief. He said that when dealing with an experienced man like him, it is hard to get away with things. He also said, "Age and experience teach you wisdom." He had two big dogs in his yard: one in front and one in back. They were strategically placed to protect the mango and genip trees in Mr. Brown's yard that attracted the boys. Mr. Brown said that anyone who wanted fruit had to ask him nicely. However, the bad boys in the neighborhood didn't bother asking. He said, "If I catch any of the boys in my yard to steal from the trees, I would beat that person and then I'd let my dog eat him for dinner."

Most of the boys knew Mr. Brown was serious. If he said something, he meant it. He often said, "A man's word is his bond. If you give your word, you should be able to keep it." Some of the guys attempted to steal his mangoes, but Mr. Brown was successful in cornering one or two of the guys not smart enough to get away. I had no problem with him and always greeted him respectfully. Sometimes I offered my help, even though I knew he would refuse it. Sometime he would call me over to chat with me about how I was doing in school. I liked when he did that. I proudly told him about my successes, and he would reward me with a dollar or two.

Now, Greg was one of my classmates who talked me into playing the revenge game of tackle football. I vowed to get him back for it one day. That day finally came when

Mr. Brown's trees were loaded with mangoes. We could see them and smell them as we passed the yard. The day before I set up the prank for Greg, I was passing by Mr. Brown's gate on my way home from school, and he called me over for one of our occasional chats. At the end of the talk, he told me to wait, and he went inside and brought me a brown bag with some mangoes inside. I thanked him, and then I hopped and skipped home as I thought about my prank. I decided to take one of the mangoes to school for Greg and tell him where he could get many more. My plan worked. I told him he could get a couple of his buddies and go to the green-and-white house on the corner of my street. I said that there was an elderly man living there, but he was not a problem. "Just open the gate, and go in. You and your friend can climb the tree and pick as many mangoes as you like."

I told him that I would stop by with a big bag he could use to carry his mangoes. He had a big grin on his face, and he licked his lips as if he had already tasted the mangoes.

We agreed to meet at five o'clock. As he walked away, I had to fight hard to keep a straight face. I knew that at five o'clock, Mr. Brown would be sitting by his window, peeking through the curtains to catch those bad boys. I couldn't wait for school to finish; I watched the clock all day.

At three o'clock, when the bell rang, I rushed out of the classroom to return a library book. And then I went to the computer lab to do some research for my science paper. Then I printed the information, thanked my teacher, and left for home. I thought about the surprise that Greg and his friends were in for, but if I had known Mr. Brown had gotten two more dogs, I might have called off the prank.

I went home, greeted my mom, changed my clothes, did my homework, and then checked the clock. I had about thirty minutes before my prank, so I ate my dinner, and then I asked Mom if she needed help with the dishes. She said yes, so I hurriedly washed dishes and then shouted, "I am going outside." I looked at the clock on the kitchen wall. The time was 4:55 p.m. I only had five minutes to hustle down to the corner.

I rushed through the gate and walked briskly down the road. As I got closer to the corner, I saw Greg and his buddies, Tony and Andy, crossing the street. They laughed loudly, pushing and shoving each other. Greg ran up to Mr. Brown's gate and opened it. He stepped into the yard, and his friends followed. He walked over to the mango tree, grabbed a limb, and swung up into the tree. One of his buddies bent down and started picking up the ripe mangoes that had already fallen off the tree. I crouched down next to a neighbor's wall so that the guys couldn't see me. But before I did that, I looked at the window where Mr. Brown usually peeked out from behind the curtain. I saw the outline of his head and then ducked quickly so he wouldn't see me. Just as I expected, Mr. Brown opened his door. Then to my surprise he let two more dogs out of his house.

The dogs rushed out, barking loudly. They ran to the mango tree and surrounded it. Mr. Brown shouted to his dogs, "Eat them alive! No one will get out alive! How dare they come into my yard and pick mangoes without asking me. If you don't eat them alive, I will finish them off with my walking stick." I moved my head to look, and I saw Greg's buddy Tony under the tree, picking up mangoes and struggling to get up into the tree, away from the dogs. But my eyes opened wider when I saw there were four dogs. Greg and Andy were in the tree, holding on for dear life. Their expressions told me they were terrified. Mr. Brown stood at the bottom of the stairs, waving his walking cane above his head. Tony had managed to climb the tree, but he went out onto the same limb where Greg and Andy were.

Suddenly, I heard a crack, and the limb broke under the weight of the three boys. Down they came, shouting, kicking, and screaming. I heard the thuds as they hit the ground. The dogs jumped on the boys, who fought to get up. The dogs were well-fed, and they pinned the boys to

the ground as they snapped at them. Mr. Brown hurried over to his dogs as he realized that what he said could become a reality. He called to his dogs and used his stick to push one off of Andy and another one off of Tony. When the boys noticed they were free, they took off limping and groaning. However, two dogs were trained on Greg, and if Mr. Brown hadn't done something fast, Greg might have been eaten alive. Greg screamed at the top of his lungs, "I don't want to die. I am sorry I tried to take your mangoes. Don't let your dogs hurt me anymore."

Mr. Brown ran over to rescue him. He raised his cane and nudged the dogs, but their teeth were tightly clenched on his clothing and maybe on some of his skin. I couldn't watch anymore, and I decided to help save my friend. I ran through the gate, I picked up a mango and threw it at the dog's head. It hit and stunned him. and then Mr. Brown grabbed the leash and pulled the dog away. Greg stood up, but the other dog was still biting his pants. Greg tried to pull away while the teeth of the other dog were still clamped onto his pants, and soon Greg's butt was exposed. His boxer shorts had been pulled down too in his attempt to escape.

Mr. Brown and I forcefully got all four dogs back into the house. I looked and saw Greg trying to pull up what was left of his pants and boxers. Both pants legs were ripped up from the wrestling match with the dogs. His arms and legs had bite marks on them. At that moment, I wanted to cry. I felt guilty. I didn't know Mr. Brown had two more dogs in the house. Greg gave me a long, hard look, and then he ran out of the gate, limping and cursing at me.

After Greg left, I sat down on Mr. Brown's steps and told him what I had done. I apologized for creating such chaos for him. He looked at me, held his head back, and laughed. He said, "Serves them right. It will teach them a lesson. Even though I was angry and scared, I had fun. My dog took the boy's drawers off! That's the best laugh I've had in a long time."

The next couple of days as I walked back and forth to school, I looked over my shoulder. After that serious prank I had pulled, I was so sure that Greg and his friends were planning something for me. At school, I was uneasy on the field or walking in the yard. The news had spread all over the school, and everyone made fun of the boys, especially Greg. He didn't say anything to me for two days, and then I decided it was time to mend the friendship. I went over to him in science class and apologized, telling him how sorry I was that he got hurt and that I missed his friendship. He softened up and accepted my apology, and then we high-fived each other and agreed to hold off on pranking each other.

Tony, Andy and Greg became friends with Mr. Brown after that incident. He was happy that he had friends to share his childhood stories and his fruit with. After school, we sometimes stopped by to help him feed and walk the dogs. However, Greg stayed away from the one that had pulled his pants down. Even now when I think about what happened that day, I smile. We encouraged Mr. Brown to sell his fruit so the neighborhood could enjoy them, and he would have more money for dog food. We helped him clean his yard and set up a fruit stand. Mr. Brown was happy and proud to tell stories about his mangoes, sugar apples, star fruit, sour sop fruit, genip fruit, and tamarinds to his customers.

MANGOS     LIMES

GRAPES     LEMONS

WATERMELON     ORANGES

STAR FRUIT     BANANAS

They enjoyed hearing the stories. The neighborhood changed after we set up Mr. Brown's fruit stand. The other neighbors met there and talked about everything. They even shared stories with Mr. Brown about their days growing up.

My friends and I were happy to help Mr. Brown pick his fruit to sell in exchange for a portion to eat. I was very pleased with the way things turned out. Everyone seemed to be getting along, and Mr. Brown loved all the attention he was getting. He said, "I am the most popular man in the neighborhood," and we all had to agree. He was not the lonely old man down the road anymore. The children and adults loved him and enjoyed his fruits. He always thanked me for doing that prank. He also thanked all the other boys who helped him set up the fruit stand.

About this time, my mind was getting restless about what my next project would be. Then I remembered that the fan in my room had stopped working. Every night before I go to sleep, many thoughts would dance around in my head.

That night, I thought about the fan. I thought, *Tomorrow, I will take it apart and find out why it stopped working.* Dad had bought that fan for me the summer before, when I complained about how hot it was in my room. I knew summer was coming up soon, and I would need my fan again. So, that was another reason I had to work on it. I had already talked dad into getting me a little tool kit.

At first he was reluctant, and when I asked him why, he replied, "I am afraid I will come home one day to find everything taken apart or in little pieces." I calmly convinced him that this would not happen, and I reminded him I needed it every day. Eventually, he gave in and bought me a tool set. I helped him do a few odd jobs around the house, and he was very pleased. I drifted off to sleep, thinking I was definitely going to use it the next day to work on my fan.

It was Saturday, so there was no school. I had all day to fix my fan. I got up, washed my face, brushed my teeth, and then went to the kitchen to find something to eat. Mom had already left to go to the market. I ate my breakfast; got up from the kitchen table and went to my room. I sat down on the bed, looked at the fan, walked over to it, plugged it in, and turned it on.

Nothing happened. I didn't see the blades turn or hear a hum. I unplugged it and went to my closet for my tool kit. I took out the big screwdriver. Next, I sat on my bed and pulled the fan closer to me, turned it around, and worked on it with my tools. I took it apart and looked at the motor. I loosened and tightened screws. I spun the blade with my hand to make sure it worked. After this, I looked at the inside parts again, and some of the wires looked frayed and burnt. I thought, *This fan is no good. It's time for a new one. These fans don't last long.*

I picked up the cord, and a tag hanging from it said, "Made in China."

That confirmed to me that it had served its time. I was just about to take the fan outside to get rid of it when Dad came to my room. "Boy, don't tell me you destroyed that fan too? What's next?"

I replied, "No, Dad! I did not mess the fan up. It had stopped working, and I was trying to fix it."

He responded, "But I just bought it last summer."

"I know, Dad! Have you read that things made in China are made cheaply? Well, I did, and that seems to be the case here."

Dad scratched his head and shook it, and then he said, "Son, we need to talk."

I replied, "Okay, Dad. I will be right back. Let me take this old fan outside." When I got back inside, my dad was sitting on the living room couch.

# Part Four

## Dad's future Plans for me/ My Choice/ My graduation

He said, "Come over here, son. You are in high school now and soon it would be time for College. Then he paused, took a deep breath and then asked, "Vendel, what do you want to study when you go to college? Before you answer, let me tell you what I have planned out. You know your uncle Bobby started out as a police officer, and he has worked and studied hard to rise through the ranks. He's captain of his command. Your other uncle, Tyrone, took a course in auto mechanics in high school and decided that's what he wanted to do. He liked working with his hands. The other day, when you started taking my car engine apart, you saw how quickly he was able to put it back together. In no time, he had my car running again. Tyrone is a well-known mechanic, and he is a smart man with a lot of skills.

"You should thank him for saving you from a beating. That day when I came out and saw you under the hood of my car, I couldn't think straight. Do you remember that afternoon?"

"Oh yes, Dad! How could I forget? You shouted at the top of your lungs. You kept saying, 'Vendel, get away from my car now! What do you think you are doing?' Then you came running down the steps at full speed. When I looked up and saw the expression on your face, something told me to run as fast as I could. I dropped the wrench in my hand and started running down the road. I heard you cursing, and I heard your footsteps behind me, so I ran faster."

I remembered that there was a shortcut I sometimes used to walk to school. I ran across the street and dashed down the trail. My heart pounded hard, and my feet hurt from the jagged stones they landed on. I saw a piece of wall I could crouch behind, and if I got to it quickly enough, you wouldn't see me. I sprinted ahead with my last bit of breath and dropped behind the wall. I curled up quietly and waited for my dad to pass. After a few minutes, I heard him panting and puffing, as he was still running at full throttle. I stayed behind the wall, hoping and praying he wouldn't find me. Ten minutes later, I heard his voice as he walked by the wall where I was still hiding. He muttered, "That son of mine has gone too far. He has destroyed everything I own. I am going to let him have it. I will not put up with any more of his experiments. I have to put a stop to it tonight."

As I crouched down there, I said to myself, "Look how my curious mind has gotten me into trouble. I should stop it." Then a second thought came to me: "Don't every stop being curious. That is how you learn things." I told myself, "You are right. You have a quest for knowledge. I will go home and talk to my father about how my natural instinct and curiosity has led me to do the things I did. I would also will accept my punishment."

I walked back to my house and saw my mom standing by the door looking sad. She came outside, put her hand on my shoulder, and said, "Don't worry, Son. Your uncle Tyrone will take care of it. I have already called him. I have also asked your dad to be patient with you.

I told him he had to allow you to explore your world and grow. I also let him know the many ways you remind me of him. He agreed with me and calmed down." A burden was lifted off my shoulders. My mom and I shared a special bond. She understood the things I did and why I did them. My mom always looked out for me and protected me.

My dad interrupted my thoughts as I remembered what had happened. "Are you listening? You seem to be daydreaming while I am trying to talk some sense into you."

I responded, "Yes, Dad! What did you say about my uncles?"

He replied, "They both wanted me to join the police force like your uncle Bobby. They said it would be a good fit for me because I was a strict disciplinarian. I made sure that they got a good education. I was the oldest of the three brothers, and I always made sure they did the right thing and followed the rules. However, because our parents died in a car accident, leaving us prematurely, I had to drop out of school and find a job to support myself and my brothers. I did what I had to do so they would have opportunities, but it changed my path. I didn't finish high school.

"I know that your Uncle Bobby would be very happy if you joined him in the Police Force. He is always looking for young officers with creative and energetic minds—just hear me out. I want you to go the New York police academy and study hard, focusing on forensics. I know you will do well. You might also do an internship at the FBI Academy. After completion of your studies, you will return here, and you will be the only one so highly trained and qualified. You will easily carve out a position for yourself. Your uncle is there to pave the way for you. What do you think about that?"

"I don't know, Dad. I need time to think about this. It is not what I had in mind."

"What do you have to think about? You are my son, this is what I want for you, and I am paying for it. I am working hard, saving all my money, to help you and ensure your success."

"Thank you, Dad, for looking out for my future. However, I still need to think things over. I must be honest with you, Dad: That is not what I want."

"What are you saying to me? You don't want what I have for you? What do you want? Think about what I am offering."

Every week after that conversation, Dad would ask me, "Have you made up your mind yet?"

I would usually reply, "Soon, dad … soon." The time was going by so fast. My high school years seemed to be going by just as fast as my middle school ones—maybe even faster.

I thought about college and prepared for it. I visited the guidance counselor often, asking her many questions. I was involved in lots of extra curricula activities, and I took AP (Advanced Placement) courses. I researched and made a list of colleges I would like to attend. I also spent time studying for and completing the PSAT. This test helped me to sharpen my skills for college and prepared me to get higher SAT scores. My teachers, my counselor, and I were pleased with my performance. I knew I was ready for college. In the back of my mind, I knew I didn't want to take the offer dad made, so I filled out a FAFSA (Free Application for Federal Student Aid). It was my backup plan in case dad got mad and withdrew his financial help. I had done a lot of research on what I wanted to do, and my success in physics and other science classes influenced my career path decision. Even though I knew this, I would wait for the right time to tell my dad. I tried to avoid him for a while. I stayed late at school, went to the library, and stopped to talk to the boys and Mr. Brown, and then I would go home when I thought my dad had gone to bed. I even got a part-time job at one of the local department stores so I didn't have to be at home as much. I didn't want to disappoint my father. I understood that he wanted to live out his dream through me, but I had my own dream to pursue. I knew we had to have a meeting of the minds and come to an understanding, and I decided I would tell him before graduation. I also decided to discuss the situation with my mom first.

So, I sat her down and told her my plans. She was very supportive, and she agreed with my decision. My mom said, "Son, we have done our best to raise you the best way we knew how, and you have reached the age of accountability. Make your own decision!" That was all I needed to hear. I knew I had made the right choice.

"Mom, I will tell Dad this evening."

I had a surprise for my mom, but I wanted it to be a guarded secret until my high school graduation day.

Mom said that she would help prepare Dad to hear my decision. She offered to cook a nice dinner, and she reminded me to get home early. During school that day, I thought about how Dad would respond. But no matter how it went, my mind was made up. I got home before Dad, so I helped my mom set the table. When Dad came in, he looked tired and dejected. Even though I was still a little bit nervous about what I was going to say to my dad; I walked over, hugged him, and said, "Hi, Dad! How are you doing? Are you feeling all right? You look tired."

He sat down, looked at me, and asked, "Have you made your decision yet?" I ignored his question.

Instead of answering, I shouted, "Mom, is dinner ready? I am so hungry, and I think dad is too."

Dad repeated his question.

I had no choice but to look at him and respond, "Yes, Dad, I have decided that I am going to engineering school. I want to be an engineer."

"What! You are not going to accept what I offered?"

Just then, Mom brought our dinner to the table placed the meal in front of us, and said, "Eat first. Talk later." My dad nodded, Mom sat down, and we all ate in silence. Then Dad got up and left the table without a word. My mom and I looked at each other, and she said, "Don't you worry, Son. I will go talk to him." I cleared the table and washed the dishes, and then I went to my room. I listened to some music.

Just as I was about to take a shower, I heard my dad call, "Vendel! Vendel!" I opened my bedroom door, and Dad stepped in and sat down on my bed. He said, "I have thought long and hard about your decision, and even though it hurt me and it is hard for me to accept, I will go along with it." I breathed a sigh of relief. Then, to my surprise, my dad stood up and gave me a bear hug. I thought he was going to squeeze the life out of me. He relaxed his grip and said, "Well, Son, you have the brain to be anything you want to be. And you have made your decision about your future. I guess I wanted to fulfill my dreams through you, but that would not be fair to you. I must give you the opportunity to be whatever you want to be. I am sorry, son, for trying to impose my will on you. You have the ability to make wise decisions and the conviction to stick to them. You are the best son a man could ask for. You have not only given me a lesson on how to be a man but also shown me how. Thank you son! You stood up under my pressure, thought long and hard, and then made your final decision. I watched you throughout those days I waited for your answer. I silently hoped you would give in and take my offer, but you didn't. You've got guts—you have what it takes to be a man. Son, I admire you, and I am proud of you."

I stood there and listened as my dad expressed his strong emotions. His words tugged at my heartstrings. In fact, tears rolled down my face when my dad hugged me. I wiped them away, but I felt comfortable in my own skin. I knew there was nothing wrong with a man crying, as it showed my humanity.

I noticed my dad was trying to hold his tears in, and then he turned his back to me to brush them away. I patted him on the back and said, "Go on, Dad. Let them fall. Be the man you have taught me to be. I will cry with you—tears of sadness and then tears of joy."

He picked up his shirt, dried his eyes, and turned around to face me. He said, "Boy, you saw me crying? I am a man. Big men don't cry." We both burst into laughter. I loved and respected my dad more after that day, and I treasured that moment.

Over the next six months, things were more relaxed at my house. I was busy sending college applications, preparing for final exams, and rehearsing for graduation! There was much excitement as I gave out invitations to the big event. All my aunts, uncles, cousins, and other relatives and friends wanted to be there. I was still holding a surprise for my parents close to my chest. On graduation day, as I marched down the aisle and heard "Pomp and Circumstance" playing, I beamed with joy. I had accomplished a lot, and most importantly, my mom and dad were proud of me. As the ceremony proceeded, my principal announced, "Let us bring our valedictorian to the podium to deliver his speech: Vendel Swanston!"

I looked out in the audience to see my mom's reaction. She leapt up from her seat, threw up her hands, and said, "Thank you, Lord! You have answered my prayer."

My father jumped up too and said, "Yes! That's our boy. Way to go, Son!" All my nervous energy disappeared as I walked across the stage proudly and delivered my speech.

I said, "Good day! Welcome to all our distinguished guests, parents, my fellow graduates, families, and friends. Thank you for sharing this day with us.

"Today, I stand before you as the happiest and proudest graduate. I became valedictorian through hard work and dedication.

"First, I would like to thank Almighty God, who has helped to make this day possible.

"Next, I would like to thank my parents. Mom and Dad, would you please stand up to be recognized? I waited for them to stand,and then I continued. They have molded me into the smart, handsome, and intelligent young man I am today."

The audience laughed and cheered loudly, and I gave my parents a well-deserved applause.

I continued, "To all my other family members and friends, thank you for your support.

"Congratulations to my fellow graduates. We came this far by faith, hard work, and prayer. We were challenged and inspired to do our best, and we did it.

"I wish to give special recognition to our teachers, our principal, and the assistant principals for imparting knowledge and wisdom to us. Also, special thanks to the faculty and staff members who nurtured and guided our path along the way."

My fellow graduates responded with shouts and applause to express the same sentiments. I felt empowered to continue my speech.

"At an early age, I was taught the importance of a good education, and I was eager to learn. I have to say a special thanks to my dad. He provided me with many opportunities to learn, and he made sure I took them."

I heard my dad shout from the audience, "Thank you, Son, for recognizing me." I smiled and kept going with my speech.

"Fellow graduates, let us take what we have learned, go out into the world, and build upon it. Don't let it be all about book knowledge. We must make sure we apply common sense too. Always remember to give back to your community. Let us move forward and make this world a better place to live. Remember, education is a key for you and me. We will continue to excel. I pray that God will continue to bless all of us.

"Thank you! Thank you!"

The applause was deafening. I walked back to my seat with my head held high and my chest puffed out. I had achieved one of my goals - my graduation from high school.

As I sat back down, I saw my mom and dad standing and applauding. I thought, *My dad is no longer mad at me, and now I know why!*

Respond to Vendel's Story

Which part of the story did you connect with the most?

What was the most interesting part?

Can you list some teachable moments (What did you learn) in the story?

# More About the Author

Patricia Maynard is a professional educator for over twenty five years.

She is very passionate about teaching and learning. She believes that all children can learn. She has taught all the Primary grades from Kindergarten to Sixth.

She was recognized as an Outstanding Teacher in the St. Thomas, St. John School District. She was also honored for her contributions to the children of the Virgin Islands.

To her credit she has made presentations at various professional workshops and organizations such as the American Federation of Teachers Mini Quest, Lockhart Elementary School Professional Day, and a Motivational Presentation to the Wesley Methodist Church Cotillion.

Her educational background includes a Bachelor of Arts in Elementary Education, Master of Arts in School Administration, Curriculum Specialist Degree and a Masters in Public Administration.

She is certified as a Highly Qualified Teacher and she also has certification as an Assistant principal.

Patricia Maynard is also very actively involved in her church and community. She is an active member of the First Wesleyan Church; a Sunday school teacher and a member of the Wesleyan Academy School board.

She is the founder of the Progressive and Ambitious Girls Club and the Know It and Grow It Boys Gardening Club

Presently she is an assistant Principal at the Joseph Gomez Elementary School.

In spite of her hectic schedule, she is committed to her family. She is married to Paul Maynard M.D. She has three sons to include a set of identical twins. Dwight, Dwayne and Paul Jr.

She is a voracious reader and she enjoys writing.